Published by Disney Press, an imprint of Disney Book Group. No part of this book may be reproduced or transmitted in any form or by any means, electronic or mechanical, including photocopying, recording, or by any information storage and retrieval system, without written permission from the publisher.

For information address Disney Press, 1101 Flower Street, Glendale, California 91201.

ISBN 978-1-4847-0300-7
T425-2382-5-13338
Printed in China
First Edition
1 3 5 7 9 10 8 6 4 2

For more Disney Press fun, visit www.disneybooks.com
This book was printed on paper created from a sustainable source

# The Royal Slumber Party

Written by Catherine Hapka • Based on an episode by Erica Rothschild
Illustrated by Character Building Studio and the Disney Storybook Artists

**Disney** PRESS
New York • Los Angeles

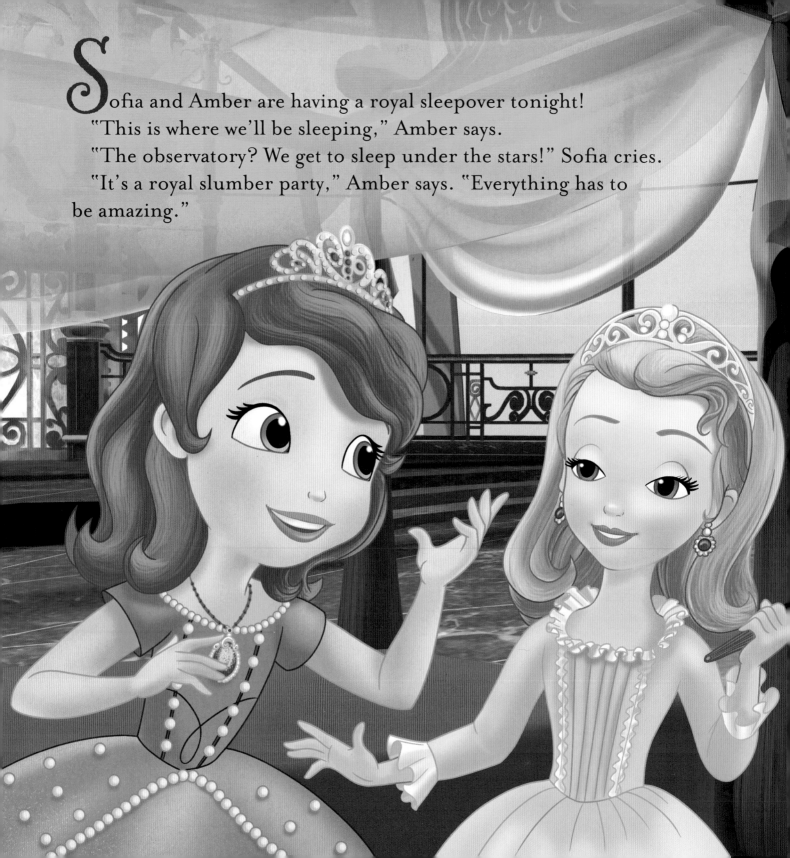

Sofia and Amber are having a royal sleepover tonight!

"This is where we'll be sleeping," Amber says.

"The observatory? We get to sleep under the stars!" Sofia cries.

"It's a royal slumber party," Amber says. "Everything has to be amazing."

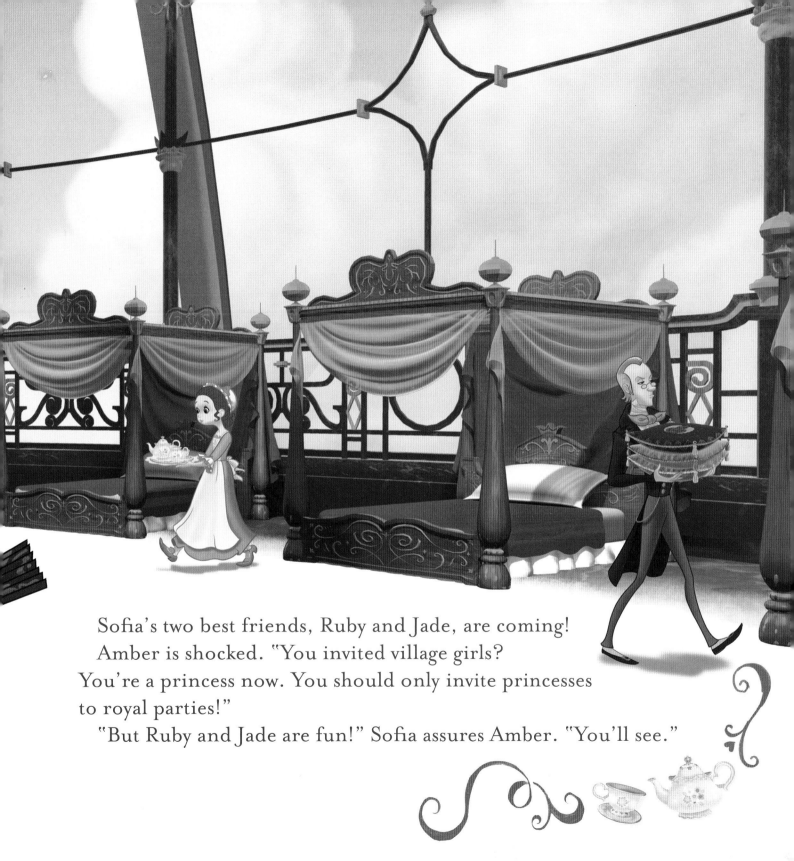

Sofia's two best friends, Ruby and Jade, are coming! Amber is shocked. "You invited village girls? You're a princess now. You should only invite princesses to royal parties!"

"But Ruby and Jade are fun!" Sofia assures Amber. "You'll see."

The royal herald's trumpet sounds. "They're here!" Sofia cries. Amber's friends, Princess Hildegard and Princess Clio, step out of their coaches. Behind them are Jade and Ruby in an oxcart. "I can't believe we're here!" Jade exclaims, hugging Sofia. "We're so excited!" Ruby adds.

It's time for the party to start! The princesses change into fancy nightgowns. Ruby and Jade giggle as they roll their hair in pinecone curlers—just like at home.

"We're at a royal sleepover!" they chant, pulling Sofia up to join their silly dance.

The other princesses stare at Ruby and Jade.
"What are they wearing?" Hildegard says.
"What are they doing?" Clio wonders.
Amber frowns. "Are those pinecones?"
Ruby hears her and dances over. "Want one?
We brought extras."

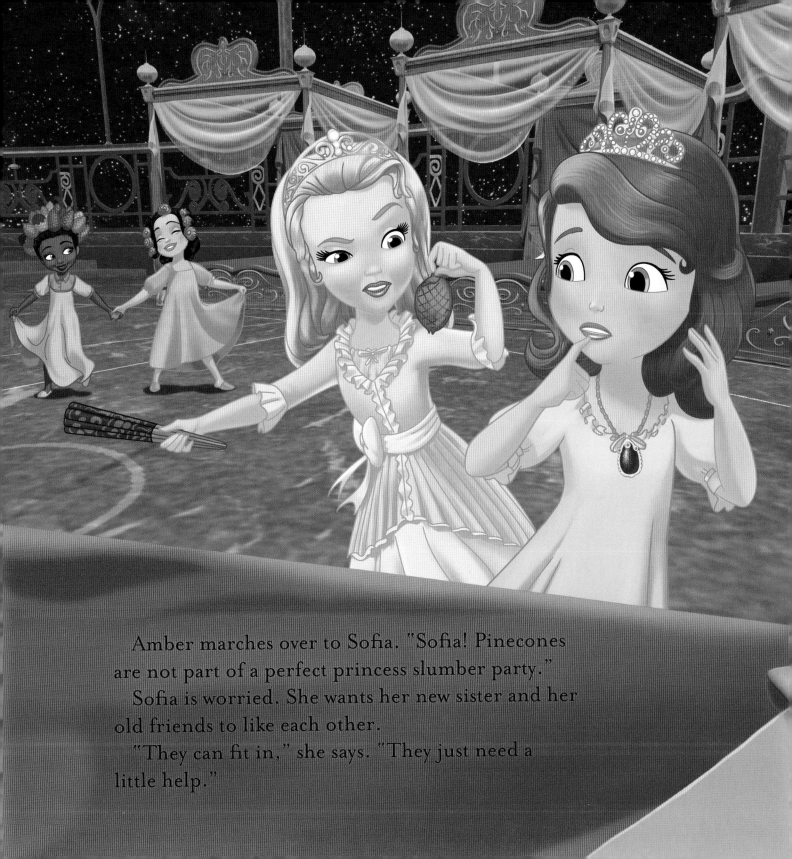

Amber marches over to Sofia. "Sofia! Pinecones
are not part of a perfect princess slumber party."

Sofia is worried. She wants her new sister and her
old friends to like each other.

"They can fit in," she says. "They just need a
little help."

Sofia has a great idea. "How would you two like a royal
makeover?" she asks her friends.

Ruby and Jade squeal with excitement!

Baileywick and Sofia's woodland friends help out. They fix
the girls' hair and dress them in pretty gowns and tiaras.

Sofia makes her friends cover their eyes. Then she leads them to a mirror. "Open your eyes," she says.

Jade and Ruby gasp when they see themselves.

"I'm a princess!" Ruby exclaims.

"Me, too!" calls Jade.

Next it's time for party activities.
First comes fan decorating.
    Ruby and Jade have fun. But their
fans don't look very princessy.

Then the girls play a game of Pin the
Tail on the Unicorn. "Ooh! Ooh!" Jade says.
"Can I go first?"
    But Jade ends up nowhere near
the unicorn!

After that, the girls watch Cedric, the royal sorcerer, put on a magic puppet show in the banquet hall. During the show, James, Sofia's brother, walks in with a message for the girls.

"Prince James!" Jade and Ruby squeal, rushing toward him. They're thrilled to see the friendly prince!

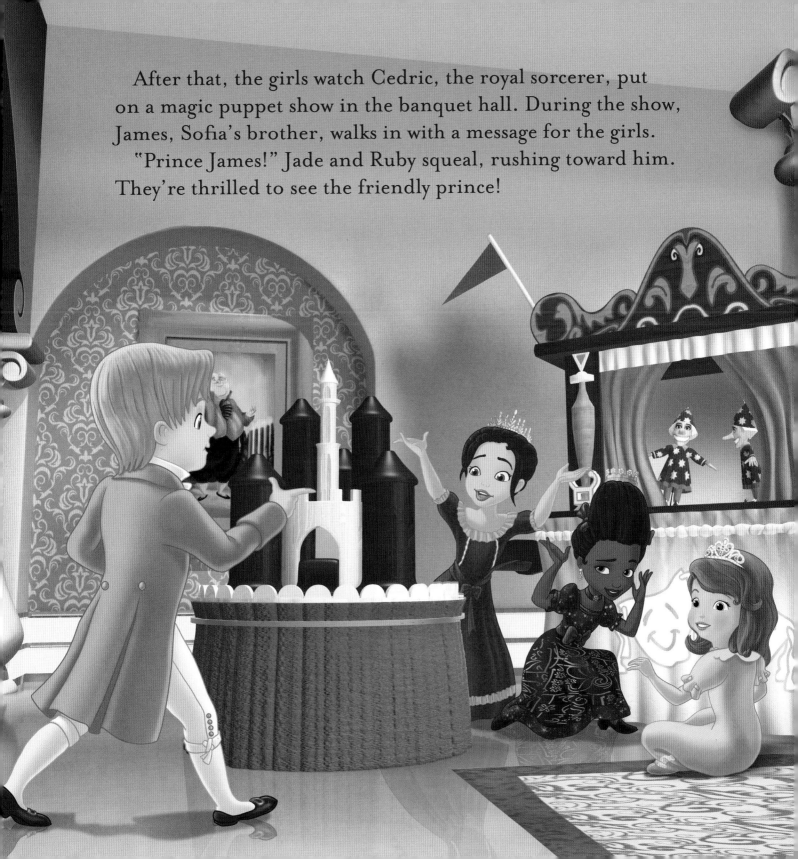

Jade and Ruby are so excited they accidentally knock over the chocolate milk fountain. Oops! Chocolate milk splashes onto Amber's nightgown. She is furious!

"We're so, so, so sorry!" Ruby says to Amber.
"So sorry," Jade adds.
Amber walks off in a huff while Sofia shakes
her head sadly.

Baileywick hurries Jade and Ruby away to get cleaned up.
Then James tells the girls it's time for dancing in the throne room.
"Let's go," Amber says. "Maybe we can enjoy five minutes of our
party without Sofia's friends making a mess."

Now Sofia's even more worried! She goes off to find her friends.

"I want you both to fit in with the princesses," Sofia explains.

"We look just like them now, don't we?" Jade says.

"Yes," Sofia says. "But princesses don't talk so much, or laugh so loud, or make so many messes."

Jade frowns. "We were just having fun."

"We're sorry," Ruby adds quickly. "We'll try to act more like Amber and the other princesses."

"Thank you!" Sofia is relieved. Now she's sure everyone will get along!

Sofia and her friends join the others in the throne room. But Ruby and Jade don't know how to waltz. All they can do is stand there and watch the princesses dance.

After a while, they tell Sofia that they want to go home.

"But you're finally fitting in!" Sofia cries. "And you're not embarrassing me anymore!"

"I'm sorry if we talk too much and laugh too loudly for your fancy new friends," says Jade. "Maybe we shouldn't be friends anymore!"

Ruby takes Jade's arm and together they rush out of the room.

"Don't worry about them," Hildegard tells Sofia. "You're with us now."

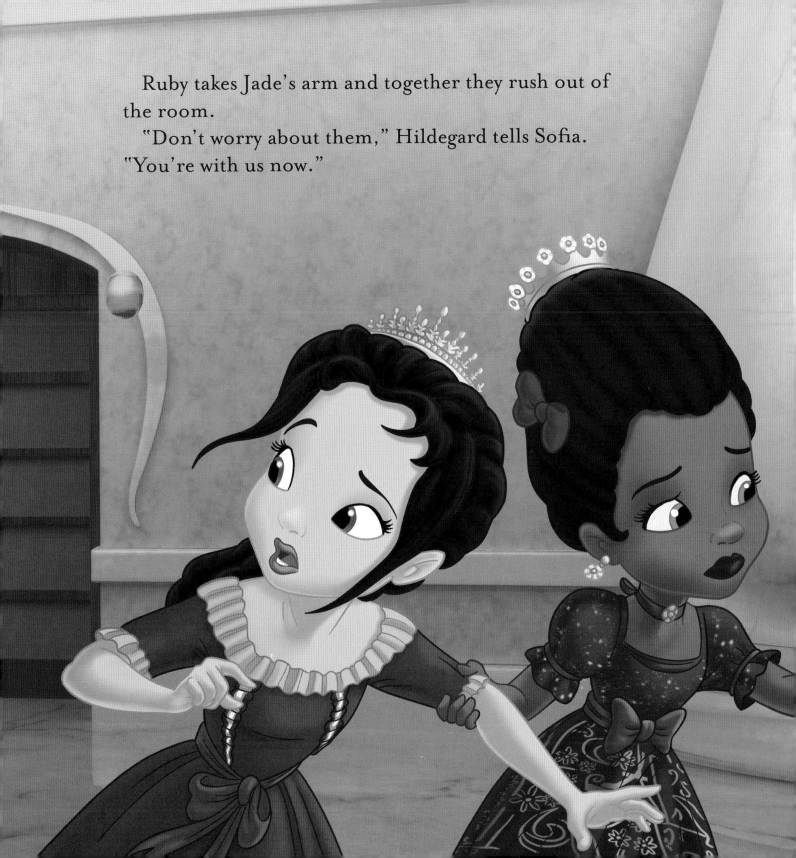

Sofia goes after her friends but finds her mother instead. "I was trying to help Jade and Ruby fit in," she explains. "But I just made them feel bad."

"A true princess treats people with kindness, Sofia," Queen Miranda says gently. "If someone is your friend, you should like them for who they are."

Sofia knows her mother is right. She runs outside and finds her friends just as they are about to leave.

"I'm sorry about the way I acted," she says. "Please let me make it up to you. We can have our own slumber party—just the three of us!"

Jade and Ruby think for a moment and finally agree to stay.

Soon Sofia and her friends are in her room, having a great time. They laugh—loudly. They talk—a lot. They roll pinecones in their hair and perch tiaras on top.

Meanwhile, Amber and her friends go back to the observatory.

"Finally, it's just us princesses," Amber says.

"This is a perfect party," Hildegard agrees with a yawn.

There's a long silence. The princesses are really bored.

"You know," Clio speaks up, "Sofia's friends were kind of fun."

A moment later, Amber and her friends knock on Sofia's door.
"Um, do you have room for a few more princesses?" asks Amber.
Sofia looks at Jade and Ruby. "What do you think?"
"The more, the merrier," Ruby says with a smile.
Sofia and Amber end up having the perfect sleepover with
friends—old and new!

# Princess Lesson

## A true princess treats people with kindness.